ODESSA
Vienna as it never was, but with sea.

David Staretz

ODESSA
Vienna as it never was, but with sea.

FOTOHOF *edition*

Scanty, funny, scabby, decayed, full of human warmth – innocent in it`s own way

ELEGY AT THE BLACK SEA

This rugged looking port city is of a conspiratorial beauty. In order to realize this, one has to confront shifted perspectives

Circus performers relax in their unique way. The beach here is called "Lang-eron" after a French governor.

The graceful girls float on high heels over the jagged, sunken sidewalks along picturesquely displaced facades. The streets, paved over for kilometers, have been adventurously re-situated over mysterious sandstone catacombs. Often they are held together by the tram tracks as if by metal staples. The blue-white tram-sets, steered mostly by women, search ploddingly along the tracks and balance joltingly over the switches. It is also mostly women who command the trolleybuses; long matte metal blocks, which flex in the middle with an accordion joint. Again and again, the drivers climb from their O-buses to hook the slipped pantograph back into its overhead guidance cable with a daring skill.

Twenty-seater minibuses, mostly used vehicles from Recklinghausen, Tübingen or Weil am Rhein, serve the standardized routes- back and forth, back and forth. The common term for this is Marshrutki (the joke usually takes a while to be understood in German).

Odessa is a port city. You only become aware of this in the winter or in bad weather when the foghorn of the lighthouse sounds. There is hardly anything sadder and at the same time more comforting than this wistful foghorn as it tones over the city at irregular intervals. Tuuuh!

We take the panoramic lift to the sixth floor of the EVROPA department store. Here you can eat cheap, the coffee is good, and if you make the effort you can see a bit of the sea above the roof of the opera house. Helmer and Fellner built the Odessitic opera, like so many theatre and opera buildings of the monarchy- Akademietheater, Konzerthaus, Volkstheater, the Ronacher in Vienna.

Odessa is not a port city with fishing nets and starfish decor in the restaurants. It lies high on a sandstone high bank, and below the loading cranes toil. Sometimes you will see a man who imitates these cranes. He has a good relationship with them. The cranes are also befriended among each other. Many are called TAKRAF. It is breathtaking when two of them lift a coal wagon on a wire cable from the rails and empty it over the loading port of a cargo ship. One man has the task of pulling the flap levers. Once there were fireworks on New Year´s Eve, with a concert stage and much noise. Stoically, the cranes continued their labor, which was touching to observe.

Up on Primorskij Boulevard one walks under year- round illuminated Platanus-Trees. Here you can stroll undisturbed and hear the women

chat about weddings and abortions; as a folk song explains. Pervij Tram-way, the early tram, also appears in this wistful song. I often heard it, at five o'clock in the morning from room 444 of the Hotel "Passage".

In the park next to the church, a man drums on pots throughout the night - quite talented. Here I also saw girls, buxom students in pairs, as they dragged Ukrainian flags filled with paving stones to the battleg-rounds of May the 2nd, 2014. We can't get past that horrible scenario, shame of Odessa, over forty deaths- all unsolved. No one dares to try for serious clarification; the events were too terrible, too deviant for the world. On the hotels television screen, a perplexed camera held up to the mob; pavement stones like snowballs and just behind the hotel the dead - dead here, dead there, one side stylized into heroes, Ukrainians all.

One might say that Odessa relates to the Ukraine like New York does to North America. Odessites love their city. "Yes, they like to say that," explains a doctor who was swimming at the Langeron beach. "But they do nothing for the city and let it fall apart! Unfortunately, she is right. Balconies, facades are crumbling; magnificent four-story houses right in the center of town are collapsing. If things don't go fast enough, one as-sists with fire by criminal intent. The last owner of the now closed Hotel "Passage" was stabbed, along with his simpatico security lad; right there in the foyer, because he stood in the way. Protective tariffs are being le-vied, partly by the policemen themselves and when the florist asserts that he has no money to pay up, Sloventij is also satisfied with a huge flower bouquet, which he passes on to Sergei, who at the moment is celebrating his 44th birthday in the dive bar "Buterbrodnaja".

Odessa is a moral, almost prudish city. The girls are so daringly pretty, that it seems provocative. Their beauty is owed to the disco-ideal and has innocence, which is difficult to explain when out of context in the streets. They are treated chivalrously. You might see men kneeling to tie their girlfriends' shoes, or to carry the girls' handbag is not an embarrassment here.

Odessa is a Ukrainian city, yet Russian is almost exclusively spoken between Romanians, Greeks, Jews, Belarusians, Albanians, Germans, Armenians, Georgians, Tatars, Gaussians, and Turks. A total of more than 150 nationalities sustain everyday life here.

Are things going well, going badly? Shrug. There are apartments, in which the rooms have a large hole in the middle, so big that you can only move around by having your back against the wall. If you look up you will find that the hole in the ceiling is just as large. In winters the schools are usually closed- heating cost savings. All public buildings depend on regionally generated heating. Regulation is done via opening the window.

If you want to complete the higher education maturity certification, you have to pay the teaching staff for it. We don't even want to talk about medical treatment. If a leg is broken, the entire extended family is financially challenged, up to the third degree of kinship. No joke.

Despite poverty and decay: Odessa is a fundamentally romantic city. You can eat and drink exquisitely here. There are hotels on an international level and great clubs, great parties, amazing musicians.

Whether on the poor or rich side, the Odessites are particularly fond of animals. Street cats can hardly finish their daily rations; fat dogs loll around in used sweaters in winter.

On Sundays we buy a grilled chicken at the kiosk and carry it to the sea. Everyone is already there: the round of well-groomed ladies, the chess players, the athletes, the circus people, the Roberts. This is what we call the Europeans and mostly Americans who were lured by internet agencies to date Ukranian girls ("My preferences: literature, picnic in the countryside, the occasional glass of wine").This is based on the essentials of romance- holding hands, large expensive brand shopping bags, and a sensual dinner with candlelight and translator. Marriage not excluded.

In 1928, Ilf and Petrow, two Odessa-born writers, published a satirical novel in which they claim that the Vorobyaninov family jewels were hidden from the Bolsheviks in one of twelve chairs. The ensuing search for the chairs scattered across the country resulted in a classic of Russian literature. Odessa secured at least a bronze statue

The emphatic passer-by thinks instinctively: "Is the pipe sick, or is it just drunk? Why does the pipe need a bucket so close by?"
The chimneys, a picture postcard motif of the lower town, can be seen in this formation from the so-called Mother-in-law Bridge

Decay is undoubtedly a certain topic here, which in many cases is followed up by complete demolition. The much-invoked romance of the city withstands minor tests.
The young man shows more solidity, as he attempts to cope with the recently more laid-back, yet traditional women

Room number 444 in the Hotel "Passage" is a suite with dusky pink silk
wallpaper and a creaky floor. The balcony can't be used due to the risk
of falling through. The room telephone works in a puzzling manner
which bypasses the fee indicator into a tariff-free zone.
Asphalt plays a major role in Odessa. After all, it often has to deal with
flexible tectonic debris or massive tree roots. Social symbolism like this
one is rarely found here

The SAS-968 Saporoshez cars were built in the 70's. They had air-cooled V4 engines mounted in the rear. Because of its distinctive engine noise, it was given the combative name of "T34-Sport". This model has peaceful intentions as a trampoline transporter

The Odessites have an uncomplicated, amiable relationship with animals. With this in mind, the worthy courtyard-guard got a hatch cut into the world

Mike Tyson looks back on a respectable filmography. He played himself in every role.
However, it is usually not mentioned that he is a passionate carrier pigeon fancier.
Odessa's streetcars are long-serving heroes of unwavering mobility

The lion in its original form can be found on the base of the statue of Catherine the Great, the founder of Odessa. The lion theme comes up often here- the ring in the mouth is suitable for dog leashes, or for decorative purposes

The Hotel "Passage" houses a hair salon and a manicure/ pedicure studio. Kolya's every day view can be seen here. His adopted son is an international martial arts master. He, himself bathes daily in the sea, and is also awaited there by stray dogs since he provides them with food

Next pages: The main actor in this vacation photo is the little dachshund on the front left. With tireless enthusiasm, he chases back and forth between the groups of people; steals a shoe here, a bathing suit there. He then tried to flirt with the little lap dog, but the owner decided to take action and grabbed the leash

Benches which have decided to go into retirement.
The changing rooms on the public beach are small mazes with tin walls.
Artists remain artists even on vacation

At the 12th Fontan, a region to the south, one finds a type of beach house unknown near the city.
Also here the coast is dealt with rather pragmatically

Upper picture: A hairstyle for two.
Below: Reduced architecture; almost inadvertently

Some courtyards are reminiscent of past beauty. Modernist boutique hotels try to use this charm in their attempt to exploit the tourists. Viktoriya (right photo) paraphrases these advertising texts as follows: "Come see father Fyodor in his historical underwear, scratching his butt on the balcony"

Undeniable advantage of a port city:
located by the sea

When the boys try their hand at the trendy sport of parcours, the girls look demonstratively bored to the side. They know- gravity always wins in the end

The following double page:
Installation in room number 444

Odessa Airport, famous for its bumpy runway. One hryvnia equals about 3 cents

What distinguishes Odessa from other modern mega-cities is its warm-hearted-
ness and the acknowledged permissiveness of everyday life. Perhaps many areas
are too poor and too amiable to be able to put on a slick façade.
Fashion plays a role

The now gone tree inscribed himself into the building's wall

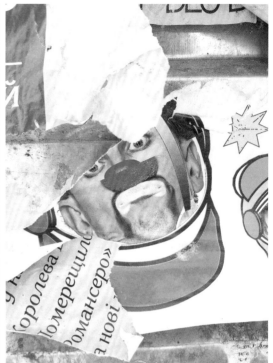

In front of the Pantelejmonovski Church, a man waits next to his Shiguli. The car sports two outside mirrors on the driver's side, and a sturdy roof rack

Viktoriya is from Novosibirsk, but by now she can give directions to the local Odessites. Her wit is sharp and to the point, but always leaves room for a sparkling joie de vivre and the good humor of the moment

One of the more enigmatic symbols of Odessa is the street
decorations. Generations of school children grow up with it,
become students and start families. When their own children
ask what it actually represents, they still don't know, but at
least think they recognize a safety pin and a belt

Places and moments, of such a defenseless and innocent manner, that one wants to cry for no reason. Given the bleakness of the moment and wretchedness of the situation, it harbors no greater yearning than the desire for it to never cease

Even novelties like
the capsized ship
seem like they have
always been there;
perhaps as part of a
tale by Isaac Babel

Anja is the receptionist at the Hotel "Passage". With a magical glance that captivates listeners, she tells long-winded stories about peculiar snail-like pets. When she recounts, with some amusement, how one of them exploded, the story still does not become more plausible for us

Schwadlenka is the name of the store for buttons and sewing accessories. Only in here, after lengthy comparisons, prolonged consultation, memories and new inspirations, can one understand how large the number of different buttons, and how wastefully long a human life can be

At Kolya's. After the haircut, you are allowed to blow-dry yourself; the next lady is waiting. They say that after Kolja's treatments, the hair grows back especially slow.
On the way to the beach one gradually becomes accustomed to the socialist style of friendliness

Katja runs the manicure studio in the Hotel "Passage". Her husband is either a night watchman, or a sailor. They own half a of a beach lot not far from the 12th Fontan

The fact that the Azerbaijani market restaurant on the second floor is a Makeshift provisional can be seen only from the outside. Inside there is no time, only substantial incidence of light

At the Starokonny, the flea market. The trappings of life are laid out in
meticulous order in the morning, and collected again in the evening

Strip club, best friends Wolf, Dog and Viktoriya; pure
colors; David Oistrakh, who was born here.
The outdoor artists defend their Œvres against
all fashions and trends

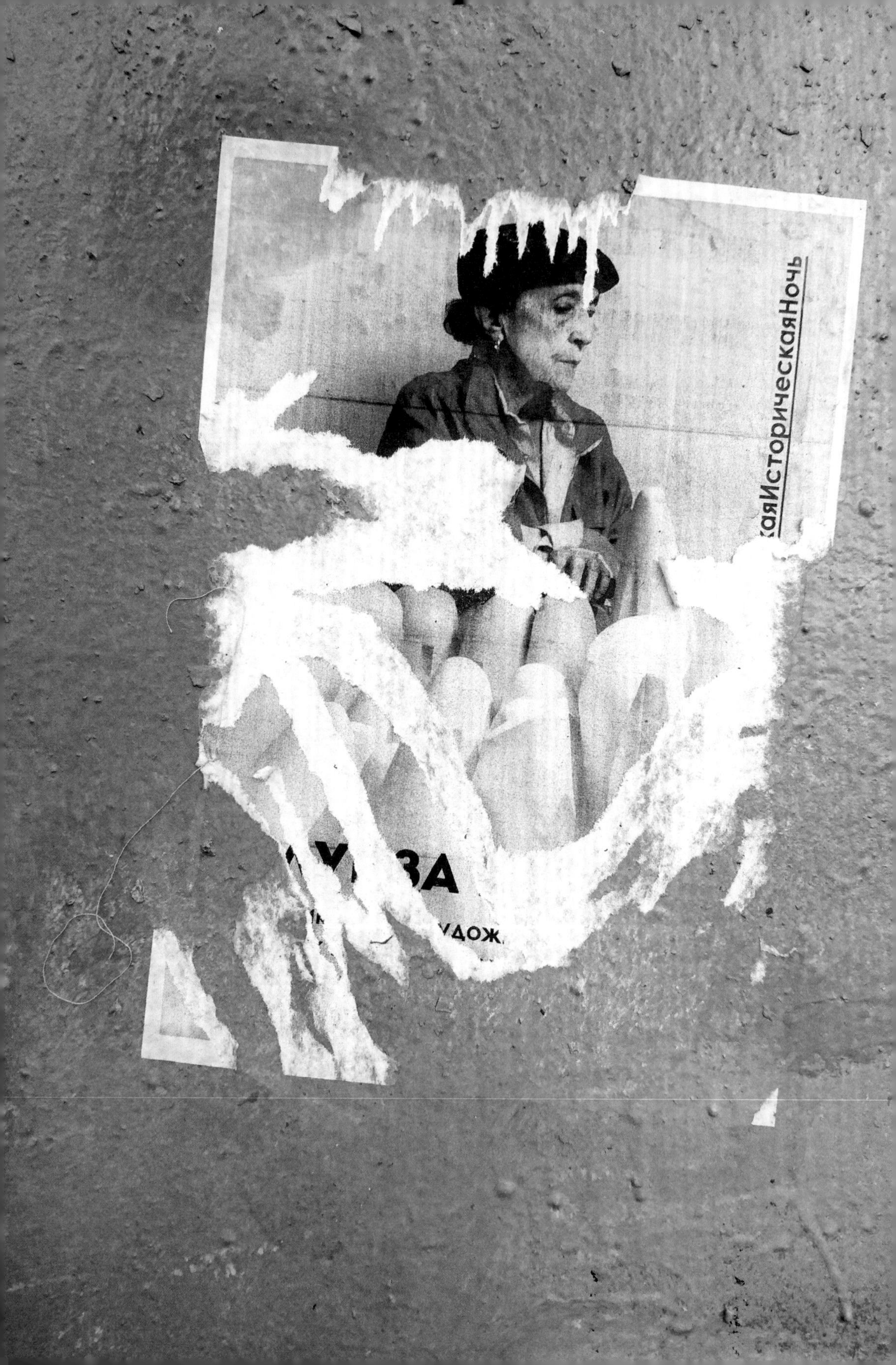

Louise Bourgeois found a good neighborhood here

Laundry bags in the Passage Hotel. Unknown artist: Mona Lisa of Odessa. Buryakov with cat Lisa in the kitchen

The horror of everyday life has many faces. Sergey, father to two unbearable sons explains: "Arsenij and Wassja quarreled so long over the oar lever, until it jumped out of the socket. Since then the boat has been stranded here"

On New Year's morning, it is a tradition to go into the water here. It is so contaminated that it never really freezes. In the spring, the metal steps are hung into place, and the swimming season begins at Langeron public Beach

The tables and benches on the beach are acting like wave barriers. In winter, they are covered with picturesque icicles. The operator of the beach kiosk stays overnight, in order to keep it from being robbed.
Electricity cables point the way

Reduced love letter out of garbage

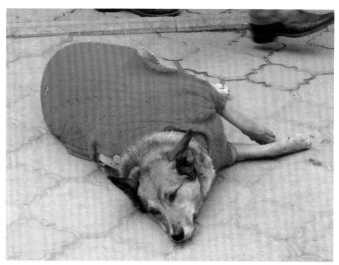

The dogs on the market wear the fashion of the previous year. Fascinating scaffolding statics. The military department at the flea market allows itself historical reminiscences

The knitted dress with the snowflake Viktoriya bought at the market „7th kilometer", which is a geographical indication. The flea market Starokonny also has a lot to offer fashiowise

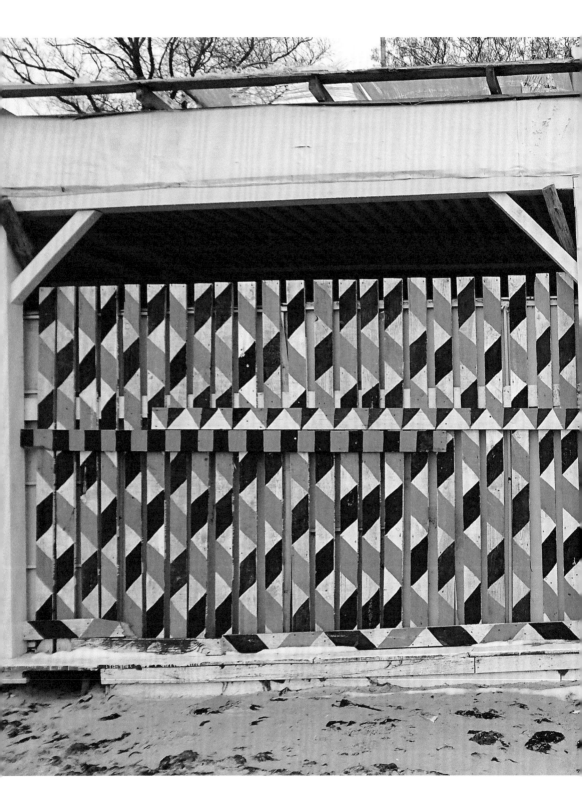

125

The musical ringing of the Transfiguration Cathedral at five o'clock
in the afternoon silences all surrounding conversations

More than a burned garbage container;
art from a loose hand is also somehow
exemplary for this city

The Morwogsal, i.e. the sea transport hall (in contrast to the Avtobuswogsal, the bus transport hall, i.e. bus station), has this tiled toilet in the basement, at about sea level

This car, an armored Alfetta 2000, was one of the convoy vehicles in which the Italian President Aldo Moro was assassinated in 1978. The car's owner recounts, "If Moro had gotten into this car, he would have survived because of the armor. But he didn't want to give up his old Fiat. That was his downfall. We had to repaint the white car to get it across the border". Now it rusts in a street of Moldovanka, the rogue district of Odessa. Moss complements it well.
Left side: architectural backwindow on a Shiguli car

Some still-lives seem to produce themselves
with such confidence that suggests an
indicator of larger arrangements

Boris Grigorevich Weiszmann is a men's tailor. He has worked for the military, for the Bolshoi Theater, and for Brezhnev. Now he stands in his "Atelier Mod" Monday to Friday and shortens jeans with disdain. With his wife, former tailoring student Tanya, he has two sons
Left: There are days when you just feel sick

From the Potemkin staircase over to the Morwagsal one has
to go up narrow stairs through a former Fiat branch.
One has, for whatever reason, renounced the magistrale

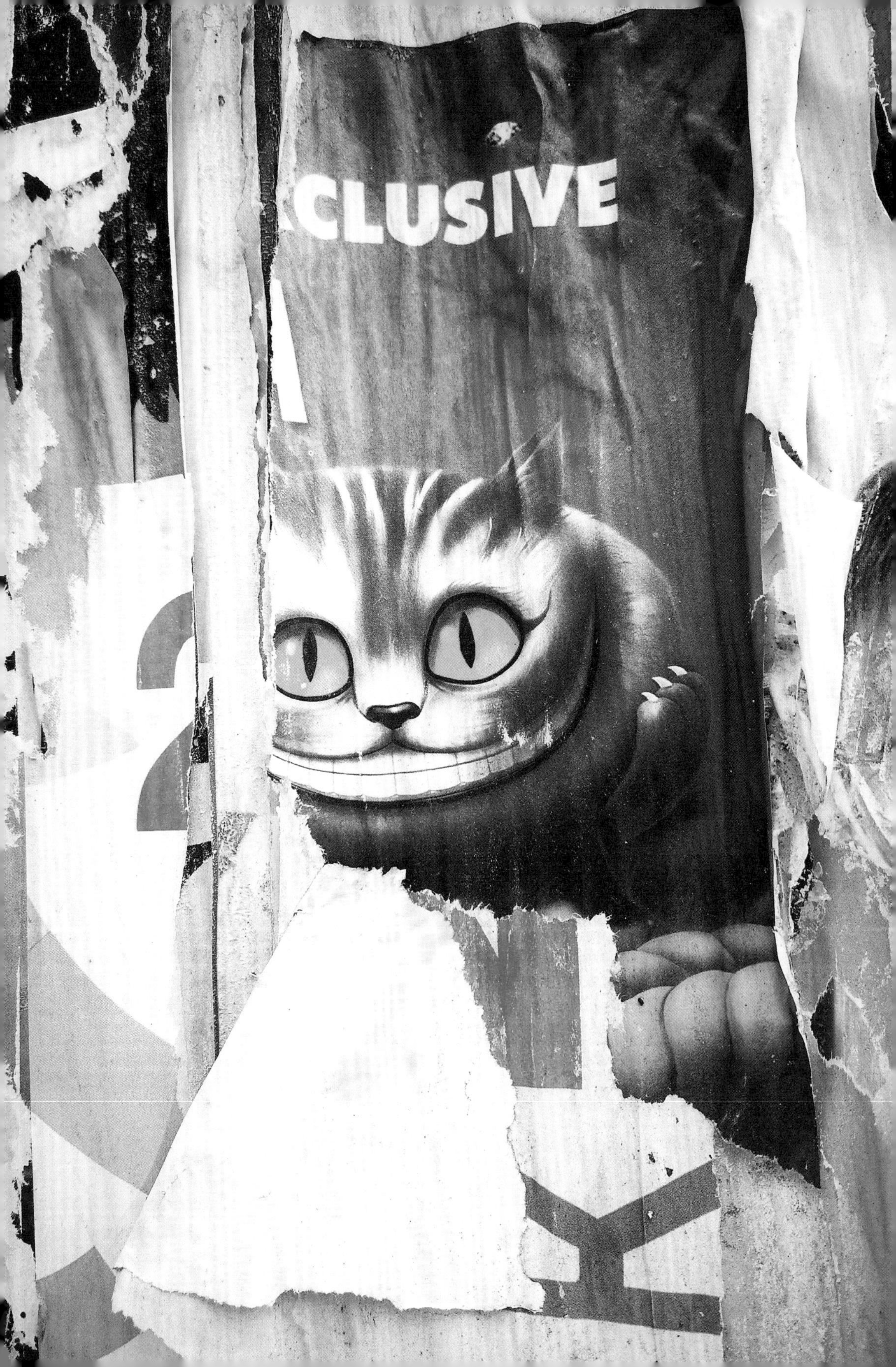
CLUSIVE

146

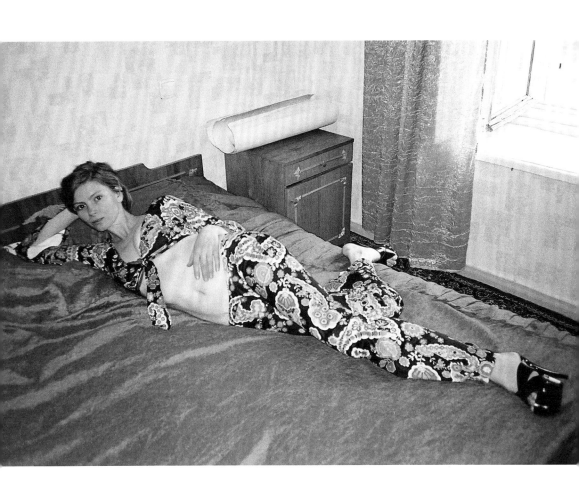

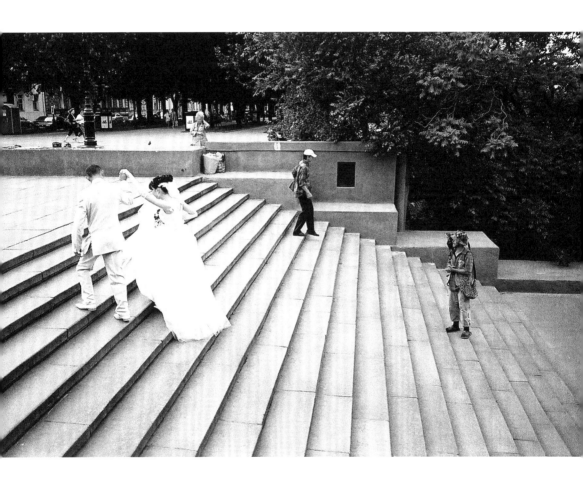

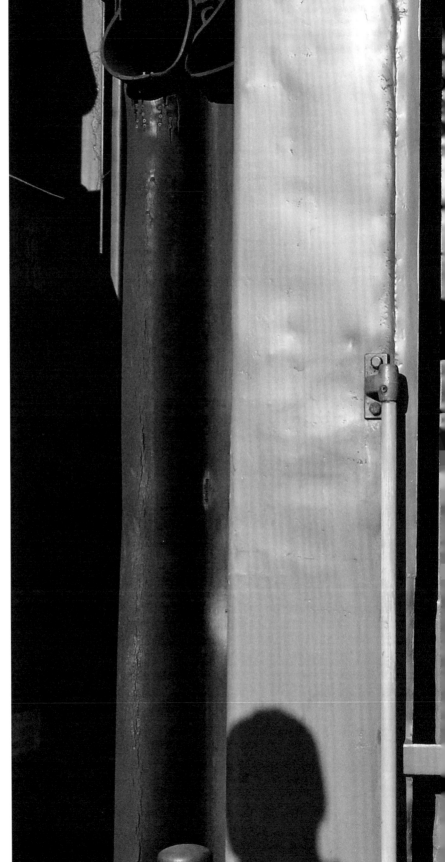

Sleeping car conductors are the captains of their railcars. They fire the stove in winter, heat the samovar for morning tea, assemble flower pots, stretch twine for climbing plants, and complain when the passengers stick to the fresh paint of the interior: "Can't you be careful? I went to such trouble!" For small sums, they rent out their own compartment in case everything else is booked out

Harbor cranes, railroads, and heavy equipment are in some way like a child's landscape. Sometimes two cranes work in unison to lift a rail car off the tracks and over the ship's loading hatch. Then levers are pulled and the cargo trickles right out of the freight car into the ship's belly

153

This well-kept Volga sedan from the seventies belongs, as you can
easily imagine, to the well-dressed gentleman on page 52

Spare parts are often difficult or impossible to obtain. In fact, it often
turns out how much on the car is actually dispensable

In the Buderbrodnaja: If you press cat Lisa in the right place,
she gleams. Barmaid Angela glows internalized.
Right: Copy of the Capitoline thorn extractor in the City Museum

A market restaurant on the second floor offers daily barbecue skewers, scumbria (mackerel), or Chatschapuri. This is white pita bread filled with fried egg and Sulguni cheese- a Georgian specialty. The fact that smoking is permitted enhances the festive mood of the location

Previous double page: In the old film and theater town Odessa, people still know a
lot about stage and costume decoration, even if it's just a kid's afternoon
Left: Cats of Odessa. They command the terrain and the love of the old ladies.
Below: Amazingly, there are graffiti movements that point out of the usual context

Hotel Tsentralnaya, three floors, no elevator

Hotel Passage. Since the owner and a security guard were murdered here in the lobby, a rupture goes through its history

Weddings are celebrated with a carnivalesque touch

Left: Iron men train here. Above: Own shadow with traffic light.
Sobaka means dog and is a feminine noun

Viktoriya, Tashaika limousine

Arseniy and his father Sergey in the kitchen of Buderbrodnaya

Viktoriya: "Don't think that all Russian women are as nice as me!"

Recruit training of the Seamen's Academy

Ibiza is the name of one of the larger open-air discos. Surprisingly, you can eat well here, too

One image for generations

In the circus foyer, there is a chair with a double seat bottom. Free tickets and change are hidden in it.
Ladies' toilet- this communication friendly arrangement is located in the "Deutsche Hausbrauerei" (German Home Brewery).
Right side: Electricity is used in the hair salon for heating purposes, just as coal or gas is burned elsewhere

Marschrutki, a parodied loanword from the German language
names the countless minibuses that travel through the city, which
you can ride for a small fee

229

Miau

The public beach has no limit as to the imaginary variety of events. Girls celebrate the evening and each other. A body builder with a stethoscope demonstrates medical skills that might benefit the young man in the right picture. Sometimes a well-dressed gentleman strides along and belts out arias at stage volume, or a beach-runner gives out shells while enthusiastically telling about the many drowning victims he saved today

On May 2, 2014, clashes broke out between pro-Russian and pro-Ukrainian groups on the occasion of a soccer match. This fire truck number one suffered a sad fate when it was pushed by the unleashed mob into the hail of cobblestones, into the fiery bursting Molotov cocktails. This black day has not been satisfactorily dealt with until today, which repeatedly drew massive international criticism. Not even the exact number of the nearly fifty dead could be determined. The fire truck is now back in service

The strangest house in town

The love of big men for small animals is a story in itself.
Like the one about the lady with the stuffed fox...

Mixing machines chorus

Sometimes misfortune has a name.
But then it is usually unpronounceable

The owner of this Shiguli has invented a perfectly
economical way of cleaning cars

The Life of Others

How to build
snowmen in Odessa

SECOND PERSPECTIVE

The Cars of Odessa, Words borrowed from German, and the Price of Youth

The men of the city go into the sea in the morning to refresh themselves, and then drink, evenly spaced, throughout the day; in the evenings they meditate over open car hoods. Girls dream walk on high heels over tectonically shattered sidewalks. Crows throw nuts at moving cars in the hope that the shells will give way. Tram tracks claim their way between uneven cobblestones, like dental braces holding broken teeth together. Massive trolley sets stumble about; find their way out of old inertia. Three men of action belabor a Shiguli with a broken wheel and heave it over the curb onto the square next to the church. The engine roars, but the tire hangs limply to one side.

A trolleybus chauffeur is fishing with a long pole for the pantographs that have tangled in the high jumble of wires. Since this is of no use, she climbs to the roof using a metal ladder at the rear of the bus to sort things out at a closer advantage. If someone honks now, everyone in the area will let you know that they also have good horns. Then the stray dogs begin to howl. A man sinks to the ground in front of the "Buterbrodna-ja" dive bar. He kneels to his companion to tie her shoe. To do this, he carefully puts down the handbag he is carrying for her and then fetches a drink for both of them in the pub garden. Most often it will be a drink of vodka, colored red with the necessary minimum of tomato juice- because of the "Kultura".

This city, which seduces me with an undeclared love, is called Odessa. It is somewhat reminiscent of post-war-era Vienna (as one would like to have imagined in a romantic delusion), but with one undeniable advantage: It is located by the sea. Which is hardly noticeable as the city is resides on a high bank. No fishing nets, no seashell trinkets in the restaurants, only the port and a multitude of loading cranes. What distinguishes Odessa from other modern megacities is its conviviality and leniency in everyday life. In many areas it is too poor and too amiable to be able to display a groomed and well-kept façade. Odessa is a city of obscure beauty. When you come home and try to tell its story, you take a deep breath- but only small episodes come out. Odessites love animals, and so you constantly meet stray cats congregating at the cat food bowls, or wayward dogs in red sweaters. A common joke reads: "If incarnation really does exist, I want to become a homeless cat in Odessa".

The city administration could not develop a strategy for dealing with the huge numbers of cars. They camp-out between the alley trees or on the sidewalks- often in rows of two or three. The lack of spare parts allows them to display their fate in pantomime by form of their missing replacement parts. The street scene is mostly dominated by nameless vehicles from the Asian region. New and used cars, swept in at the time when the banks were loaning money, but today, the repayment is becoming increasingly unlikely. German limousines with darkened windows, Range Rovers, or Lexus coupes roar over the pavement boasting of new money and quick fortune. An absurdly low-lying BMW three-seater, frog green with blue headlights, searches for pot holes in the brittle asphalt. The white stretch limos, popular at weddings, are conveniently long enough to stretch from the registry office to the church.

Odessa was founded 225 years ago on the orders of Catherine the Great. Clever governors like the French duke Armand de Richelieu created

the conditions for the flourishing of handicrafts, economy and culture. The port developed into an essential gateway to the west, infusing the region with all sorts of western goods (and sailors from all over the world), even in communist times. The city was always influenced by the Mediterranean; culturally mixed and open to the foreign- occasionally involuntarily. Unfortunately, the city simply could not accommodate the masses of cheap imported cars.

Modern new buildings are shooting up. Opaque Mafia-like projects, which despite the glazing remain non-transparent, stand in a sharp contrast to the old buildings in the Kaiser-Anniversary-style with their damp, crumbling facades and collapsing balconies. The inner courtyards look picturesque, but are basically poor and neglected, like so much in the communal area. If it snows, private garbage removal units have to be dispatched. In the central city area, every street is a paved and tree lined avenue. Here you can still see the urban planning spirit of Tsarina Katharina's pioneers. Modern lifestyle shops operate branches for the rich clients that are abundant here. Many of the products are fakes, which in a Slavic port city are folklore; here you will find Lagerfeld branches that the namesake has never heard of. It is similar with Guess? Bruno Banani, Benetton, Tommy Hilfinger or Trussardi. In most cases, the following applies: counterfeits can be recognized by their price, but even this rule can only be applied to a limited extent- surprises are possible in both directions.

Most of the public transportation occurs in boxy buses. Yellow, white, ocher, lavender or plastered with advertising; they sometimes refer to Osnabrück or Sendling from where they were retired years ago. They are named by a puzzling derivative of dialect "Mauschroutiki"; the Germanic association arrives like a belated punch line. Similar words: "Platzkart" (for a cheap bunk in a sleeping wagon) and of course "Buderbrodnaja - butter bread" for the grunge bar. There the Russian Viktoriya and I have breakfast in the midst of happy alcoholics, whose grouping and mood will hardly change by dinner-time. Looking for other words associated with German: Zifferblat (the dial of a clock),

Buchalter (bookkeeper), Lobsig (fretsaw),

Schlagbáum (railway crossing barrier), Stammestka (chisel),

Straf (fine or punishment), Stangenzyrkul (bar circle, caliper), Stempel (official embossed stamping tool), Schaiba (a disk), Mundstuck (mouthpiece).

Viktoriyas Mother calls. She has just travelled from the "Chinterland" to the Crimea with the "Platzkart" and is looking for the best parúkmachér (hairdresser) in a "Churort" (resort town). The specifically Odessite idioms also contain loanwords from Ukrainian or Yiddish. It is spoken softly, often as a curse, but with a friendly base note, that suggests the tone of childlike innocence. Once a man on the street asked me to tie his tie- he had to go to the registry office.

Wolga, Shiguli,Moskvitch or Lada- the stock of old vehicles is looked after here, like only in Cuba. You certainly can tell from their looks that they don't belong to the bank. To keep it this way, they are often used for little side jobs. With a knowledgeable local lady at my side, I am spared the obligatory taxi fee for foreigners, and soon, at the wave of the hand a red Shiguli hobbles up. In an Austrian recollection these cars register as Fiat 124. A 4-door vehicle, manufactured as a licensed product in Togliattigrad in the Khrushchev era; it is automatically understood as a car with ride- sharing options. No need for a taxi symbol, a taximeter or carpooling initiative. Quickly one comes to an agreement on the fare, which is somewhere between ten and forty Griwna, depending on whether you only want to go to the nearest market or to the train station (Wagsal) , Langeron beach or the modern shipping pier (Morwagsal). Thus, you pay between one and 4 Euros. The chauffeur, by type a "fiend", as my companion classifies massive jar heads in leather jackets, starts to rock like a marine diesel, which indicates that he is laughing hard (Viktoriya had shared her favorite joke*). The initial audacity of his driving maneuvers is soon reduced by the dilapidated suspension and the destructive character of the road surface. Most of the times, these reptile-thick leatherjackets reveal

---

*) Victoriyas favorite joke, the one with the dead police men, who float down the river, cannot be told in public. Her second favorite goes like this: Raoul Castro shakes his dying brother: "Fidel, wake up again, millions of people are here, they want to say farewell!" Fidel replies: "Oh yes, where do they want to go to?"

a touching romantic at the core. With tender care the cog-gears of the transmission are merged with a long shift lever and the generous play in the steering causes his hairy paws to perform an interlacing dance. Sad Odessitic tunes swirl the dust from the speaker boxes onto the hat shelf. The text reveals lines like: What do the women talk about on Primorsky Boulevard? About weddings and abortion…" Here to listen to: http://www.youtube.com7watchßv=C1HTBR7jKAU&feature=related

Soon the Shiguli reached the grand market "Seventh Kilometer", which lies in a corresponding distance to the city. A container settlement, where absolutely everything is available for the purchase.   A certain pride forbids us to pay for the return-fare, which is triple, the amount of a self-organized journey. Thus, I step onboard a cheap microbus and I am rewarded by the astonishing phenomena of Russian warmth and a lively coziness. I experienced this before in the moss-sealed log cabins of Moldavia or an icy winter's journey in a coal heated sleeping coach with its plant-décor and Samovar Tea. Much like the used Mercedes busses; livened up with a warm cordiality and an alert bustle of people, who often have some real problems, not like those we think we have at home.   There are thickly wrapped Babushki in their heavy stove pipe Walenkie-Felt-boots next to a delicate tall young woman, who would be called a top-model elsewhere. One sees the teenagers with earplugs and cables that disappear into the adventurous depths of their fake Fantasy designer jackets, while the shoulder brushes up against heavy older men with solemn faces. As soon as the bus is full, we can depart. We all sway to the beat of the potholes, as they strike a song from the suffering coil springs, much like the singing prongs of a music box. As we circumnavigate various vehicles bogged down in the mud, my companion explains that the desolate place we are going through is called in translation "Not Boring" and that we are on its main street, namely the "Not Boring Street". As we disembark, every passenger silently places a banknote valued at about 20 cents near the driver – The chauffeur now says to my friend who inadvertently did not pay for me: "Djewushka, doesn't the young man want to pay?" With a bright red face, I put down the two-Grivna note. Youth has its price.

It's quite simple. You just have to remove all the defective parts